Contents

I want you now.
(Tennant-Lowe)

Losing my mind.
(Stephen Sondheim)

If there was love.
(Tennant-Lowe)

So sorry, I said.
(Tennant-Lowe)

Dont drop bombs.
(Tennant-Lowe)

Twist in my sobriety.
(Tanita Tikaram)

Rent.
(Tennant-Lowe)

Love pains.
(Price-Walsh-Barri)

Tonight is forever.
(Tennant-Lowe)

I can't say goodnight.
(Tennant-Lowe)

© 1989 10 Music Ltd.

101-109 Ladbroke Grove, London W11 1PG.

Photocopying of this copyright material is illegal.

Exclusive distributors:
International Music Publications
Southend Road, Woodford Green
Essex IG8 8HW.

© Cage Music Ltd/10 Music Ltd for the world.
Australia: Virgin Music Australia (Pty) Ltd.
Belgium, Luxembourg: Virgin Belgium Publishing NV/SA.
The Netherlands: Virgin Benelux Publishing BV.
France: Editions Virgin Musique.
Germany, Austria, Switzerland: Song Edition.
Virgin Schallplatten GmbH & Co KG.
Greece: Virgin Mousikes Ekdosis Eterias EPE.
Italy: Edizioni Musicali Virgin Dischi Srl.
Scandinavia, Finland, Iceland: Virgin Music AB.
Spain, Portugal: Virgin Espana SA.
USA, Canada: Virgin Music Inc. (ASCAP).
Virgin Songs Inc. (BMI).

Book designed by 3a.

Photography by David La Chapelle.

Printed by Panda Press, Haverhill, Suffolk.

I want you now

Words and Music by
TENNANT/LOWE

Rent

Words and Music by
TENNANT/LOWE

9

10

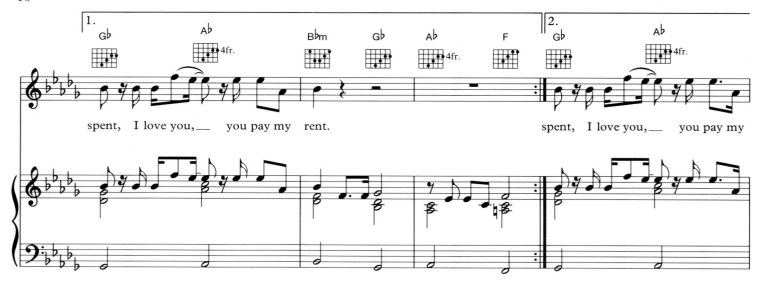

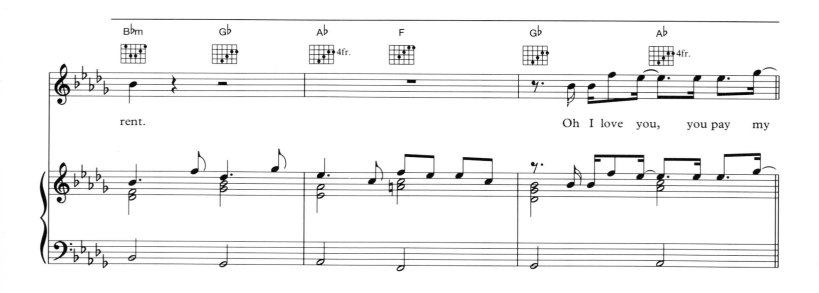

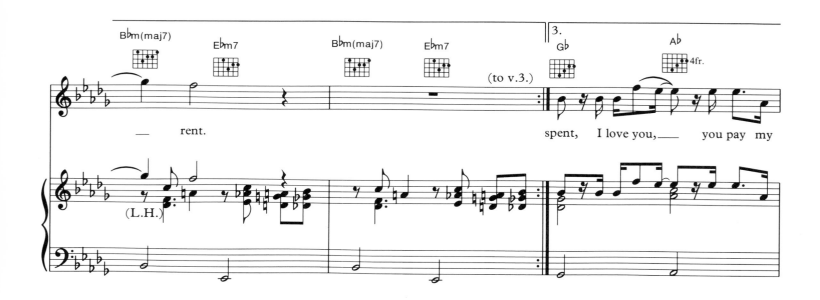

I can't say goodnight

Words and Music by
TENNANT/LOWE

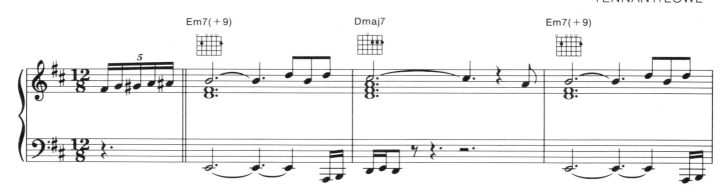

1. I don't know whe-ther   I'll love you much lon - ger
2. I don't know whe-ther   I need you so bad - ly
3. I don't know whe-ther   I'll love you much long - er

I don't know whe-ther,_____   whe-ther I can
I don't know if___ ev-er,_____   if ev-er I did
I don't know whe-ther,_____   whe-ther I can

Don't drop bombs

Words and Music by
TENNANT/LOWE

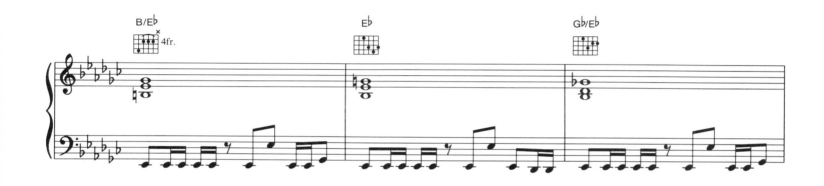

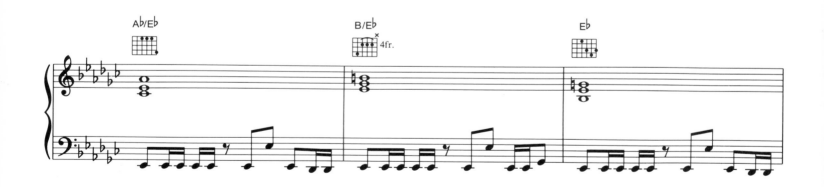

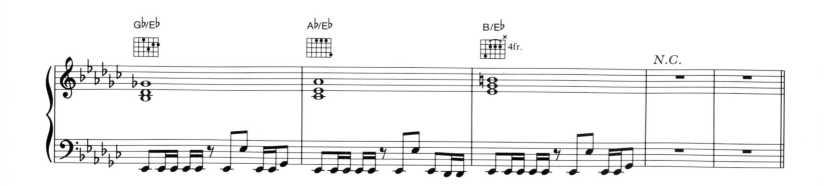

© 1989 Cage Music Ltd. / 10 Music Ltd., 101–109 Ladbroke Grove, London W11 1PG

So sorry, I said

Words and Music by
TENNANT/LOWE

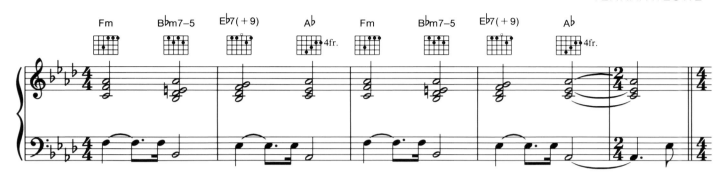

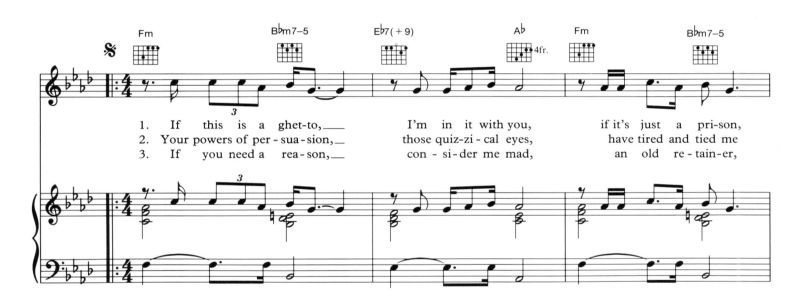

1. If this is a ghet-to,___ I'm in it with you, if it's just a pri-son,
2. Your powers of per-sua-sion,___ those quiz-zi-cal eyes, have tired and tied me
3. If you need a rea-son,___ con-si-der me mad, an old re-tain-er,

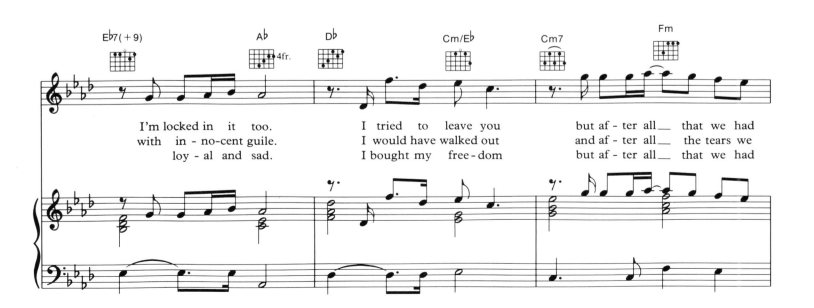

I'm locked in it too. I tried to leave you but af-ter all___ that we had
with in-no-cent guile. I would have walked out and af-ter all___ the tears we
loy-al and sad. I bought my free-dom but af-ter all___ that we had

If there was love

Words and Music by
TENNANT/LOWE

1. Men of af - fairs,   wo-men with   pow - er,_
2. Poll-sters and   plan-ners   in-cre - di - bly   sad
3. There's a hole   in the sky   as dis-tant and   vast

3rd time to Chorus

sa - tel - lites   talk-ing   to clut-ter our _____ lives,
in - del - ibly   ink-ing   their names a-cross our _____ lives
as our moral   va-cuum   and grow-ing as   fast_

banks   of pre - dic-tions,   po - li - cies   made,
in - di - vi-dual   free-dom   in - trin-si-cally   curbed

28

SPOKEN PASSAGE: Sonnet 94 By William Shakespeare

They that have power to hurt and will do none
They that do not do the thing they most do show
Who, moving others, are themselves as stone
Unmoved, cold, and to temptation slow;
They rightly do inherit heaven's graces
And husbands nature's riches from expense;
They are the lords and the owners of their faces

Others but stewards of their excellence
The summer's flower is to the summer sweet,
Though to itself it only live and die;
But if that flower with base infection meet,
The basest weed outbraves his dignity:
For sweetest things turn sourest by their deeds;
Lilies that fester smell far worse than weeds.

Love pains

Words and Music by
PRICE/BARRI/WALSH

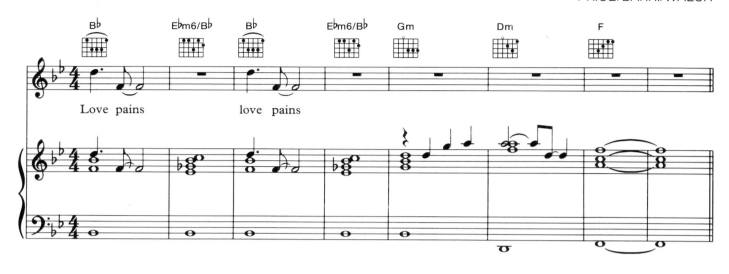

Love pains   love pains

love   pains

1. Mid - night,_   I watch you as you're sleep - ing
2. Can't   help,_   can't help but re - mem - ber

© 1979 Warner Chappell Music Ltd

you don't know I'm leav - ing, my bags are packed to
the love we had so ten - der,

go, oh___ no,___ no, no. It hurts me,
sound, oh___ no,___ no, no. His kiss,

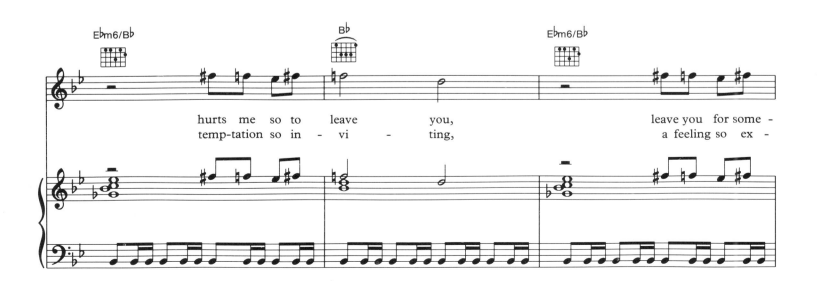

hurts me so to leave you, leave you for some -
temp-tation so in - vi - ting, a feeling so ex -

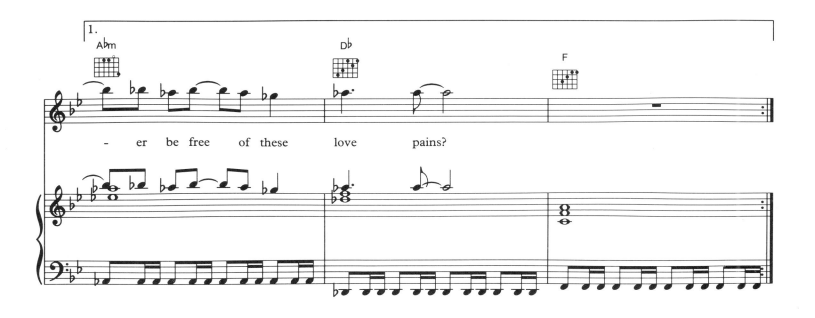

34

Tonight is forever

Words and Music by
TENNANT/LOWE

© 1986 Cage Music Ltd. / 10 Music Ltd., 101–109 Ladbroke Grove, London W11 1PG

We don't need a - ny - more when we dance,

and we'll think of the fu - ture to - night.

Losing my mind

Words and Music by
STEPHEN SONDHEIM

40

42

Twist in my sobriety

Words and Music by
TANITA TIKARAM

Ad. lib rap

1. All God's child-ren need tra-vel-ling shoes,
2. In the morn-ing when I wipe my brow,
3. We just poked a lit-tle emp-ty pie,
4. I don't care a-bout their dif-fer-ent thoughts,
5. Half the peo-ple read the pa-pers,

drive your prob-lems from here. All good peo-ple read
wipe the miles a-way, I like to think I can
for the fun the peo-ple had a night. Late at night don't need hos-
dif-fer-ent thoughts are good for me. Up in arms and
read them good and well, pret-ty peo-ple,

© 1988 Brogue Music / Warner Chappell Music Ltd

46

Printed in England
Panda Press · Haverhill · Suffolk • 3/90